Dedication

For William and Joshua.

Part 1: The No Uniform Day

Bungo Bear woke up one sunny morning with a sparkle in his eyes. It was a special day at school a "No Uniform Day" where everyone could wear whatever they wanted. Bungo Bear's mind raced with excitement as he rummaged through his colourful wardrobe. He had the perfect idea!

Bounding downstairs, Bungo Bear found his dear Grandpa Pooh sipping honey tea at the kitchen table. "Grandpa Pooh!" he exclaimed, unable to contain his excitement . "Today is no uniform day! I want to wear my favourite pink T-shirt to school!"

Grandpa Pooh paused, a puzzled look on his face. "Oh, Bungo, boys don't wear pink," he said looking worried "It's a colour for girls, you know."

Grandpa Pooh's words upset Bungo Bear "but why Grandpa Pooh?" He asked "pink is a great colour, it's bright and makes me feel happy ".

Part 2: Bungo Bear's Colourful Friends

Despite Grandpa Pooh's harsh words, Bungo Bear set off to the woods, determined to discover the truth about if some things are just for boys and others just for girls.
As he walked through the enchanted forest near his home, he stumbled upon a clearing where a group of colourful characters awaited him.

First, he met Lily the Lioness, who jumped into the clearing, dribbling a football with ease. "Hey there, Bungo! Who says girls can't play football?" Lily asked with a cheeky grin. Bungo Bear's eyes widened, seeing that Lily was just as good at football as any boy.

Next Harper the Hedgehog appeared, wearing overalls and standing next to a beautiful painting "I love to paint and draw" she said. "Arts and crafts aren't just for girls. Boys can enjoy them too." .

As Bungo Bear walked deeper into the forest , a flurry of movement caught his eye. It was Sam the Squirrel, leaping and twirling with grace and ease. "Dancing is my groove," Sam chattered as he jumped and skipped around. Bungo Bear couldn't help but join in, it made him feel happy and carefree.

Lastly, Maya the Monkey swung down from the trees, holding a magnifying glass in her hand "I love bugs and spiders" she smiled. "Not all girls find them gross. I think they're sweet". Bungo Bear was not so sure. "I'm not a fan of creepy crawlies. But these butterflies are pretty" he said.

By the end of his walk through the forest Bungo Bear had met many new friends. They had opened his eyes to new ideas and shown him that despite old beliefs, boys can be sensitive and enjoy peaceful fun. He also learned that girls can be adventurous and join in with all the games that people thought were just for boys.

Part 3: Grandpa Pooh's Awakening

As Bungo Bear continued his colourful adventure with Lily, Harper, Sam, and Maya, his heart filled with joy as he tried new things and learned being your true self helps you live your best life. Meanwhile, back at home, Grandpa Pooh couldn't shake off the conversation he had with Bungo Bear.

Deep in thought, Grandpa Pooh stared at the old family photographs on the walls of their cozy den. Young Bungo Bear had seemed quite upset being told that his pink t-shirt was something for a girl. All this nonsense was very hard to understand. Boys wear blue, girls wear pink. Boys like being competitive and having adventures. Girls are quiet, artistic and calm. It's how it's always been. It's good enough for grandpa Pooh, it was good enough for his dad and his dad before him. It's just how things are and should be.

Suddenly, a thought struck Grandpa Pooh!" That boy needs my help to show him what's what. I will go on a quest of my own, then I can show him the error of his ways and keep him safe from being bullied and laughed at".

With his mind made up to get to the bottom of this madness, Grandpa Pooh set out on an adventure of his own. He looked for answers, read books and spoke to some of his wisest friends. Oliver the owl told Grandpa Pooh all about his granddaughter Olivia. "She has never liked wearing dresses and would rather spend her time building things in the shed instead of playing with her dolls". "Not very ladylike" said Grandpa Pooh "you must be very disappointed". "Not at all" said his friend "She's happy and healthy. Also we can spend time together making things. It's nice to share an interest".

Mr Orangutang chatted to Grandpa Pooh about his nephew Oscar "He loves to bake and cook". "Oh dear" said Grandpa Pooh "the shame of it. What a girly thing to do!".
 "Not one bit!" His friend replied. "The cakes and pies he makes are delicious. He has won prizes and I'm very proud of him. I'm sad I never learned to cook like that but it wasn't the done thing when we were young".

Part 4: The Joyful Reunion

Bungo Bear returned home, his heart was full of joy. He had learned new things and made some great new friends. He walked into the cozy den to find Grandpa Pooh waiting for him with warm smile on his face.

"Grandpa Pooh!" cried Bungo Bear, rushing into his open arms. "You won't believe all of things I've learned and the amazing friends I've made.".

Grandpa Pooh was so glad to see Bungo Bear, Holding him tightly in a huge bear hug. "I've missed you, my dear Bungo," he said. "And I have something important to share with you as well.".

Sitting down together, Bungo Bear and Grandpa Pooh told each other about where they had been and what they had learned. Grandpa Pooh apologised for upsetting Bungo Bear. "I thought I was keeping you safe from harm and protecting you from being laughed at" explained the older bear. "I went on an adventure of my own to prove my point, but I learned I was wrong. I'm so sorry. Can you ever forgive me?".

Bungo Bear listened to his grandfather, he saw that Grandpa Pooh was truly sorry and learned the error of his ways. With a gentle smile Bungo Bear told Grandpa Pooh, "It's okay, Grandpa. We all make mistakes, but what matters is that we learn and grow from them.

From that moment, Bungo Bear and Grandpa Pooh made a promise to each other to spend more time together, respect each other's beliefs and to encourage others to do the same. They decided to share what they had learned with the whole community, helping everyone to break free from old beliefs, respect each other's feelings and live their best lives.

As word of Bungo Bear and Grandpa Pooh's journey spread throughout the community like wildfire. All the animals gathered for a special event at the public stage in the forest clearing eager to hear the inspiring tale for themselves.

Bungo Bear and Grandpa Pooh stood together on the stage. Taking turns they told the whole story, from the argument that started it all to the joyful reunion and the lessons they had learned.

As Bungo Bear and Grandpa Pooh told their story the other animals listened and learned. Parents began to see how sometimes old ideas and beliefs aren't always right. Just because things used to be one way, that as we learn and grow they can change and everyone should be free to express themselves and do what they enjoy.

One by one, children and adults stepped forward, sharing their own stories of breaking old rules and embracing a colourful world. Boys danced happily, wearing pink jumpers and t-shirts.Girls played football with confidence, wearing their favourite team's kit. Everyone had a wonderful time doing the things they enjoyed Just like Bungo Bear and his friends had shown them.

Once the story was finished Grandpa Pooh hung an old sheet at the back of the stage. Harper the Hedgehog handed out paints and brushes to all the animals. Everybody came together to create a mural, a bright colourful painting that celebrated the lessons that Grandpa Pooh and Bungo Bear had shared with them.

As night fell and it was time to go home, Bungo Bear and Grandpa Pooh stood in front of the finished painting. It had been a busy day. They had learned important lessons and made some great new friends. They left the mural on display as a reminder of what they had learned and returned home for a lovely cup of honey tea.

Thank you for reading Bungo Bear's Colourful Adventure.

Bungo and his friends will be back for another story soon.

About the author

Thank you for choosing this book. Where to start? At the beginning I suppose. Growing up my dear departed Nana would tell me that one of my ancestors was an Irish village storyteller (apparently a real job at the time). She also told me I was a direct descendant of the ancient kings of Ireland (but that is a story for another day).

We are a creative family with a strong drive to educate and entertain people. My Mum is a retired teacher, my younger brother as well as now having a career in education has also had a strong interest and successful involvement in the performing arts, my cousin has a great job in television and has also done some amazing charity work, my grandfather was a Newspaper man and my Dad taught people how to drive as well as serving our local community as a town councillor and did many other interesting jobs.

It's no surprise that I have always wanted to do something informative and creative. After a string of jobs that I never really enjoyed I've finally settled into a career in public service, which I love but that creative bug still gnawed away at my soul.

Fast forward to January this year. While everyone else is looking forward to a new year finally free from the shadow of the recent pandemic. I find myself in Papworth Hospital waiting to be cut in half like Debbie McGee. A routine check up had revealed a serious medical condition, which untreated could kill me. While everyone else was tucking into left over turkey sandwiches and pickles I was beginning a long road to recovery.

Given this second chance and having the opportunity to re-evaluate my life lead me to the decision to finally do something I had always wanted to and write a book. At school I never really fitted in with any particular group, never brilliant or overly troublesome. For that reason I flew under the radar for pretty much the whole of my academic career. Cool kids shunned me, bullies ignored me and most of my teachers were unaware that I was even in their class. My circle of friends was always small but incredibly tight and this is a trend that has followed me into later life. I realised that nobody wrote books for children like I was. So this is what I have tried to achieve with the Bungo Bear series. These books go out to all the kids at the back of the class, the slightly odd and easily forgotten.

So remember, we are all individuals, everyone counts and we are never too old to learn and grow. I hope you enjoyed this book. X

Printed in Great Britain
by Amazon